THE ADVENTURES OF

written by
ANTHONY J. McCABE

illustrated by
MARION JOHNSON

from an original idea by Anthony P. McCabe

Published by Fiordland Books
Riverton, Southland, New Zealand

ISBN 0 473 01456 4

Printed by Craig Printing Co. Ltd, 67 Tay Street,
Invercargill, New Zealand. 1993 — 101700

© 1993 Fiordland Books

In the beginning Sheewee didn't have a name. He was called Nobody and he lived with his family in a cave high in the mountains.

Sometimes he would climb to his favourite place on top of a high rock and sit in the sun dreaming of the day when he would have a *real* name — a name of his very own.

Nobody was older than his brothers and sisters and in the summer while they played amongst the rocks and tussocks he worked hard helping his parents gather berries and juicy tussock ends for their winter food.

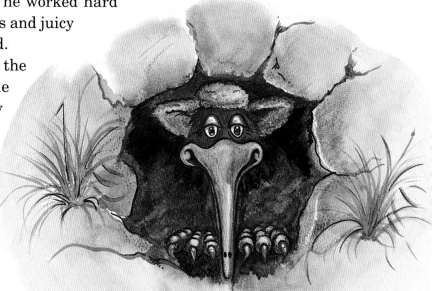

For when winter came and the snow lay deep and frozen on the mountains they all had to stay safely in their cave where they were warm and dry.

One day as winter was ending Nobody stood at the door of the cave and stared longingly at the Forest far below.

He was feeling sad and restless.

"What is the matter with you Nobody?" asked his mother who was snipping off juicy tussock ends with her strong beak. "Why do you look so sad and restless?"

"I don't have a name, Mother," said Nobody sadly. "Why is that?"

"Name!" said his mother with a puzzled look on her face. "Whatever makes you ask such a question. We are Nobodys and Nobodys have no names," and she gathered up a bundle of juicy tussock ends and hurried into the cave.

So Nobody asked his father, "Who am I, Father? What is my name?"

And his father replied, "What foolishness is this! Why should you have a name?"

"The Kea told me, Father. He has a name and Deer have names too. Stag told me he has always been called Stag."

But his father muttered, "Nonsense . . . Nonsense. We Nobodys have no use for names," and he went on pulling a tussock to pieces with his strong beak.

Nobody then asked his grandmother and his grandmother said with a twinkle in her eye, "Something tells me you are going to try to find a name for yourself no matter what I say," and she carried on bundling up the tussock pieces his father had pulled out.

So Nobody went to look for his grandfather and found him sitting in the sun the way Nobodys do when they are very old.

"Grandfather," said Nobody, "please tell me why I don't have a name."

"Others are Somebodys and Somebodys have names. We Nobodys have never had names and we are none the poorer for it."

"But I want a name, Grandfather," said Nobody.

"Then never will you find a name here," said his grandfather with a frown, "for there are none to be found."

"Then I must go and find a name for myself," said Nobody with a determined look on his face.

"Ah!" said his grandfather nodding his head. "Once I had the same idea but never did I go, so never did I get there."

Nobody was silent for a long time while he thought of what his grandfather had said.

"I will get there, Grandfather," said Nobody, "and I will start my journey this very day."

4

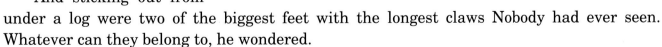

And so it was that Nobody left home to find a name for himself. Now he was tired for he had come a long way and the Forest lay before him shining green and strange in the afternoon sun.

Nobody felt just a little scared. It wasn't at all like Kea had said it would be. There didn't seem to be anyone about. Perhaps if he called loudly someone would answer. And he lifted his head and whistled loudly, "Whee-eee-oo."

Nobody listened carefully but there was no answer. He called again but still there was no answer and he was just about to give up when he heard a voice calling faintly from the edge of the Forest.

"Help me," cried the voice.

"Help me please."

Nobody jumped down from the rock he was standing on and ran to a small clearing on the edge of the Forest. "Where are you?" he called.

"Where do you think I am?" said the voice. "I'm under here and I'm stuck."

And sticking out from under a log were two of the biggest feet with the longest claws Nobody had ever seen. Whatever can they belong to, he wondered.

"What are you waiting for?" said the voice under the log, sounding decidedly grumpy. "Get me out of here."

"I'll pull you out," said Nobody and standing on his two back legs he took a strong grip of one large foot and PULLED.

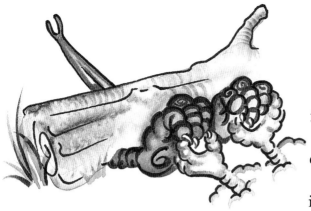

"STOP! STOP!" shouted the muffled voice.

"Sorry," said Nobody politely. "Did I hurt you?"

"You nearly pulled my leg off," said the voice from under the log.

"I'll dig you out," shouted Nobody and began digging furiously.

And so hard did he dig with his strong legs that it wasn't long before the log came loose.

"I'm going to lift the log now," he called, "so you can get out."

"Well, get on with it," said the voice, sounding grumpier than ever.

Nobody lay on his back and wriggled under one end of the log. Then with his four feet and claws gripping the log he pushed upwards as hard as he could.

Slowly the end of the log lifted and then there was a great commotion as a large body covered with dirt and moss shot backwards out from under the log and tumbled head over heels into the clearing.

Nobody let go of the log and scrambled to his feet. Then he jumped back in alarm as the owner of the voice rose to its feet and shook itself vigorously sending dirt and pieces flying all over the place.

Nobody looked up at the rumpled figure in front of him. It had feathers . . . long feathers, and a beak . . . a huge beak, much bigger than his own and small brown eyes that blinked at him.

"What . . . what are you?" he asked in a small voice.

"What do you mean WHAT am I. I'm Kiwi . . . everybody knows that . . . I live here." The figure shook itself again and leaned forward to peer at Nobody.

"The question is," said the Kiwi, "What are you?" and his long beak reached out and prodded Nobody gently. "I've never seen one like you before . . . Um . . . what do you call yourself?"

"Nobody," said Nobody a trifle nervously.

"Nobody!" exclaimed the Kiwi in surprise. "Don't you have a proper name?"

"No," said Nobody and hung his head in shame.

Kiwi looked down at the small figure in front of him with a puzzled frown.

"Hmmmm," he said thoughtfully, "So you don't know who you are or what your name is." Nobody shook his head.

"Well," said Kiwi in a friendly tone, "I don't know who you are and I must confess I don't know what you are either. But I dare say we will find out soon enough. Umm . . . where do you come from?"

"Up there," said Nobody pointing to where the sun was still shining on the tops of the mountains. "All the Nobodys live up there."

"That's very odd," said the Kiwi. "Well come on then, we can't stand here. It will be dark soon and we need a place to sleep . . . Are you hungry?"

"Oh yes," said Nobody eyeing the long tussocks in the clearing. "But I will soon find something to eat," and he began pulling a big tussock to pieces and snipping off the juicy ends just the way he did at home.

Soon he had quite a heap of pieces and these he scooped up and tucked under his beak.

"Well I'll be blowed," said Kiwi shaking his head. "Well I'll be blowed."

And with that the new found friends set off side by side down a track that led deep into the Forest.

* * *

Shortly before dark Kiwi showed Nobody a hollow under a large rock where they could sleep and as they settled down Kiwi said kindly, "Well my young friend . . . tomorrow we will try to find out who you are and then perhaps we will find a name for you."

"Do you really think you can find a name for me?" said Nobody excitedly.

"With a little help I'm sure I can," said Kiwi. "I know all of the animals in the Forest and I am sure they will want to help. For instance there's Goat . . . he's always eating and he's as fat as a pig but he gets about and hears things . . . and he's a good fellow in a funny sort of way. Yes . . . Yes, I quite like Goat.

"And then there's Pig. He's quite a character is Pig. If anything he's fatter than Goat and he's covered in big orange and black spots. But he knows a lot, does Pig."

"Then there's Stag and Doe Deer . . ."

"I know Stag," said Nobody sleepily.

"And there's Sheep," Kiwi went on. "He comes from the mountains too, you know, though he spends a lot of time in the Forest. And of course there's Owl and Pigeon and Kaka . . . and Tui . . . and others too."

Kiwi paused and looked down at the strong little figure beside him with its funny rounded ears and thick woolly, or was it furry, body, and then he smiled because Nobody was snuggled up against him, fast asleep.

* * *

Now it just so happened that the first animal they met in the morning was Goat and Goat as usual was eating. But he stopped eating as he saw Kiwi and his companion approaching and said with his mouth still full of clover, "Whassat?"

"Good morning to you Goat," said Kiwi, "and what do you mean Whassat?"

"What is Whassat?" said Goat staring at Nobody in astonishment.

"I take it that you have never seen anyone like my young friend before," said Kiwi gruffly for he felt that Goat was being rather rude.

Goat shook his head and said nothing.

"I WAS going to ask if you know who he is," said Kiwi.

"Uh . . . Uh . . . doesn't he know who he is?"

"I'm afraid he doesn't," Kiwi said with a frown. "But we are going to ask everyone in the Forest until we find out." And away they went down the path leaving Goat mumbling to himself between mouthfuls of clover.

They hadn't gone far when they came upon Kaka sitting on the branch of a tree in the sun. "I'm sorry," said Kaka in his harsh voice, "I really can't help you," and stretched his

glossy green wings showing the beautiful colours underneath.

"Why don't you ask Pig," he said. "He might know something," and away he flew whistling and screeching and carrying on the way Kakas do.

"That," said Kiwi shaking his head, "was Kaka. Not all that interested was he."

Nobody shook his head doubtfully.

"Cheer-up," said Kiwi giving Nobody a friendly rub with his beak. "Let's go and find Pig."

But when they found Pig he was fast asleep in a bed of ferns and when Kiwi prodded him with his beak he just flapped an ear and grunted.

"WAKE UP," Kiwi said loudly and kicked Pig gently with his foot.

"Oi," said Pig opening one eye. "Can't you let a fellow sleep," and promptly shut his eye again.

Kiwi was annoyed. "I've a good mind to give him a real kick," he said and drew back his leg to do just that.

"Please don't bother him," said Nobody quickly. The thought of Kiwi really kicking that huge body scared him.

"Oh, very well," said Kiwi reluctantly. "Perhaps you're right." And then turning his head to one side he said, "I can hear Pigeon and Tui. Let's see if they can help."

But when they asked Pigeon and Tui if they knew who Nobody was OR if they had ever seen anyone like him, their answer was the same. They had never seen anyone like Nobody.

"I wouldn't like to say what he looks like," croaked Frog from the edge of a nearby pond and plopped back into the water.

"Don't really know," said Drake who had paddled to the edge of the pond. And he tipped himself bottom up and head down in the water.

"I think he looks lovely," said Duck as she tipped up too.

"Oh dear . . . what shall we do now?" said Nobody looking quite sad.

"I know what to do," chattered a voice and Kiwi and Nobody looked up to see a furry face and a pair of big sad eyes staring at them from a hollow tree. It was Possum and he had the best idea of all.

"I heard what you were saying," chattered Possum, "and I have an idea. I think you should ask Owl. I mean if he doesn't know what a Nobody or a Nothing is I'm sure he will know how to find out."

Kiwi nodded his head. "That's a splendid idea Possum. And thank you for your help. We *will* ask Owl but first we must find him."

"I will find Owl for you," twittered a voice from close by. It was Fantail who, as usual, was flitting about in his bright, inquisitive way.

"Tell Owl to come to the clearing," Kiwi called out as Fantail flitted quickly into the trees.

"Well, come on then young fellow," said Kiwi cheerfully, "let's be on our way," and Nobody gave a happy skip and a jump as they set off down the path.

* * *

When Kiwi and Nobody arrived at the clearing in the Forest they sat in the sun beside the big stump that stood in the middle of the clearing and waited for Owl.

Very soon Owl appeared with a swish swish swish of his wings and landed on the stump beside them.

"TUT TUT TUT," said Owl when he heard what Kiwi had to say. "Such a strange thing . . . such a never to be heard of thing. A fine young fellow like this without a name! We must do something . . . Now let me see. What . . . can we . . . do?" And Owl blinked his eyes in a wise sort of way. "I know," he said. "We must call a meeting straight away . . ."

"An excellent idea," said Kiwi looking around the clearing. "As a matter of fact I think most of us are here already."

"I don't want to make a nuisance of myself," Nobody said looking alarmed and moving close to Kiwi.

"Come, come," said Owl opening his eyes wide at Nobody. "Don't be scared. A meeting is nothing to be worried about. Isn't that right Kiwi?"

But before Kiwi could answer, a mournful voice answered for him.

"A meeting is not what I want."

It was Goat who was sitting under the big berry tree staring longingly at the berries shining red and plump high above him.

"Oh Ooh, Oooh, I'm so hungry," he said rubbing his fat stomach. "I'm starving," and he groaned in a most convincing way.

"Would you like some berries?" asked Nobody.

"Oooh yes . . . yes please," said Goat looking at Nobody hopefully.

"Then let me help," said Nobody and jumping down from the tussock he was sitting on he ran to the berry tree and scooted straight up it. At the top he picked a bunch of the juiciest berries and tossed them down to Goat and then ran straight down the tree again.

"Well, I do declare!" exclaimed Kiwi looking very pleased and proud.

"MOST unusual . . . in fact most extraordinary," Owl said and raised his eyebrows to show how surprised he was.

"I just know we are going to be friends," mumbled Goat as he began eating greedily.

"Don't eat them all," said Pig trotting up in a hurry.

"Go away Pig," said Goat eating faster than ever.

"As I was saying," hooted Owl above the commotion, "we are going to have a meeting . . ."

"Oh dear, oh dear," said Goat as Pig pulled the bunch of berries away from him.

"That's who we need," screeched Kaka from the berry tree.

"Who, who?" asked Owl sounding just a little peeved.

"Deer of course," chortled Kaka. "Doe Deer and Stag must be here for the meeting . . . and Pigeon and Tui."

"I'm here," said Pigeon from the branches above. "And I'm here too," piped Tui from the topmost branch.

"And that's the lot I think," said Kiwi thinking how nice it would be to find a cool, dark place and rest a while. "I really could do with a sleep," he said blinking his eyes wearily.

"A splendid idea," agreed Owl. "I think I could do with a sleep too." And as he flew off into the Forest he called out at the top of his voice, "Everybody be here for the meeting."

Nobody was so excited he ran around a rock so fast he raised a cloud of dust. He raced across the clearing and jumped into a large tussock and disappeared. Then, as all the animals said "Oooh", he popped up again.

"We Nobodys and Nothings can hide as quick as can be," he said and laughed so happily everyone laughed with him.

* * *

Late that
afternoon all of the
animals began to gather in
the clearing.

Kiwi had found a cool, dark place to have a
sleep in and he was looking refreshed and quite his usual good-
natured self again.

Goat just happened to be sitting under the berry tree and Pig was beside him scratching
himself on a log. And sitting just above them in the berry tree were Kaka, Pigeon and Tui.

The rest of the animals were gathered around the stump in the middle of the clearing on
top of which sat Owl looking very dignified and important.

"Ahem," said Owl loudly. "AHEM," he said louder still and all of the animals stopped
talking so they could hear what Owl had to say.

"What we need," said Owl solemnly, "are ideas about what to call our young friend
Nobody. I think we all agree that to call him Nobody is most unsuitable indeed."

And all eyes turned to Nobody who did his best to hide behind Kiwi.

"I've got an idea," said Goat. "Let's call him Berry Getter."

"I knew it would be about food," said Owl in a pained voice.

"What about round and rounder or little bounder," rasped Kaka from the berry tree.

"Oi, even I know you can't call him round and rounder or little bounder," grunted Pig.

Owl flapped his wings impatiently. "Some sensible suggestions if you please," he said sternly.

There was a moment's silence and then from the shadows under the trees a small clear voice said, "I have a suggestion."

"Quiet everyone," said Kiwi pointing with his beak. "Doe Deer has something to say."

When the talking had died down Doe Deer began to speak.

"I think we all agree that Nobody looks a little like Kiwi," she said.

The animals nodded in agreement while Kiwi mumbled, "Well, I suppose you could say that . . . just a little . . . "

"His beak is like Kiwi's," Doe Deer went on, "and I think that like Kiwi he is handsome too."

"Oh, come come, Doe Deer," Kiwi said in a pleased sort of way. "I'm not really handsome you know . . . "

"WE know that," shouted Goat gleefully to giggles and laughter and even Owl had to turn his head to hide a smile.

"He's got a lovely coat," continued Doe Deer.

"A bit like old Sheep over there," chortled Goat who was now having the time of his life and enjoying all the attention he was getting.

"I'm not like him am I?" Nobody whispered to Kiwi.

"Not really," Kiwi whispered back, "although Sheep has a lovely warm coat and so do you."

But there was no stopping Goat now.

"He's got legs and feet like Kiwi," he called out, "but he's got more of them!" And he laughed so hard he had to lie down and thump his fat sides to get his breath back.

"Well, he won't be getting you any more berries from the top of the berry tree and neither will I," scolded Kaka.

Poor Goat! At the thought of no more berries he stopped laughing and his long face became longer still and very sad.

Suddenly there was a loud THUMP as Stag stamped his foot on the ground. "Listen to my lady," he said in his deep voice. "She has more to say."

Doe Deer looked thankfully up at Stag who stood tall and strong beside her.

"I was saying that Nobody looks a lot like Kiwi in a nice sort of way and a little like Sheep also in a nice sort of way . . . and that's how I think we can best give him a name."

"Woolly Kee . . ." sniggered Goat before he could stop himself.

"Oh dear . . . I'm sorry, Nobody . . . really I am."

"Woolly Kee doesn't sound right at all," croaked Frog from the rushes.

"He's a happy fellow and he should have a happy name," said Owl wisely.

And then there was a long silence while everyone tried hard to think what Nobody's name should be.

Finally it was Kiwi who spoke. "Well . . . ah . . . let me see now . . . We all seem to agree that my young friend here looks a little like Sheep and a little like me . . . so I thought perhaps we might call him Sheewee . . . What do you think?"

Sheewee . . .   Sheewee . . .

    the name was murmured and muttered and passed around until smiles appeared and the animals began to nod and chuckle as the name sounded better and better.

    But it was Nobody who made the name his own.

    "I'm not Nobody any more," he shouted joyfully. And he jumped high into the air and turned over twice before he landed on the ground.

    "I'm somebody . . . I'm somebody," he cried and raced around and around the tussocks in a cloud of dust. "I'm Sheewee . . . I'm Sheewee!" he shouted and raced right up to the top of the berry tree and back down again.

"Go back up again and get some berries," pleaded Goat and all of the animals hooted and squawked and croaked and laughed so hard they nearly cried.

And some of them did cry a little too because they were so happy for Nobody — who was Nobody no more.

"Thank you Kiwi, thank you Owl, thank you EVERYONE!" shouted Sheewee happily. And he raced back up the berry tree to pick a bunch of berries for you know who.

. . . THE END

In our next story, Book Two, Sheewee and Stag race through a storm to rescue Owl from danger.